RUSKIN BOND

GREAT STORIES FOR CHILDREN

Volume 4

MOONSTONE

Published in Moonstone
by Rupa Publications India Pvt. Ltd 2023
7/16, Ansari Road, Daryaganj
New Delhi 110002

Sales centres:
Prayagraj Bengaluru Chennai
Hyderabad Jaipur Kathmandu
Kolkata Mumbai

P-ISBN: 978-93-5702-391-7
E-ISBN: 978-93-5702-445-7

First impression 2023

10 9 8 7 6 5 4 3 2 1

The moral right of the author has been asserted.

The Girl on the Train

I had the train compartment to myself up to Rohana, then a girl got in. The couple who saw her off were probably her parents; they seemed very anxious about her comfort, and the woman gave the girl detailed instructions as to where to keep her things, when not to lean out of windows, and how to avoid speaking to strangers.

They said their goodbyes and the train pulled out of the station. As I was going blind at the time, my eyes sensitive only to light and darkness, I was unable to tell what the girl looked like; but I knew she wore slippers from the way they slapped against her heels.

It would take me some time to discover something about her looks, and perhaps I never would. But I liked the sound of her voice, and even the sound of her slippers.

'Are you going all the way to Dehra?' I asked.

I must have been sitting in a dark corner, because my voice startled her. She gave a little exclamation and said, 'I didn't know anyone else was here.'

Well, it often happens that people with good eyesight fail to see what is right in front of them. They have too much to take in, I suppose.

Whereas people who cannot see (or see very little)

have to take in only the essentials, whatever registers most tellingly on their remaining senses.

'I didn't see you either,' I said. 'But I heard you come in.'

I wondered if I would be able to prevent her from discovering that I was blind. Provided I keep to my seat, I thought, it shouldn't be too difficult.

The girl said, 'I'm getting off at Saharanpur. My aunt is meeting me there.'

'Then I had better not get too familiar,' I replied. 'Aunts are usually formidable creatures.'

'Where are you going?' she asked.

'To Dehra, and then to Mussoorie.'

'Oh, how lucky you are. I wish I was going to Mussoorie. I love the hills. Especially in October.'

'Yes, this is the best time,' I said, calling on my memories. 'The hills are covered with wild dahlias, the sun is delicious, and at night you can sit in front of a logfire and drink a little brandy. Most of the tourists have gone, and the roads are quiet and almost deserted. Yes, October is the best time.'

She was silent. I wondered if my words had touched her, or whether she thought me a romantic fool. Then I made a mistake.

'What is it like outside?' I asked.

She seemed to find nothing strange in the question. Had she noticed already that I could not see? But her next question removed my doubts.

'Why don't you look out of the window?' she asked.

I moved easily along the berth and felt for the window ledge. The window was open, and I faced it, making a pretence of studying the landscape. I heard the panting of the engine, the rumble of the wheels, and, in my mind's eye, I could see telegraph posts flashing by.

'Have you noticed,' I ventured, 'that the trees seem to be moving while we seem to be standing still?'

'That always happens,' she said.

'Do you see any animals?'

'No,' I answered quite confidently. I knew that there were hardly any animals left in the forests near Dehra.

I turned from the window and faced the girl, and for a while we sat in silence.

'You have an interesting face,' I remarked. I was becoming quite daring, but it was a safe remark. Few girls can resist flattery. She laughed pleasantly—a clear ringing laugh.

'It's nice to be told I have an interesting face. I'm tired of people telling me I have a pretty face.'

Oh, so you do have a pretty face, thought I; and aloud I said, 'Well, an interesting face can also be pretty'.

'You are a very gallant young man,' she said 'but why are you so serious?'

I thought, then, I would try to laugh for her, but the thought of laughter only made me feel troubled and lonely.

'We'll soon be at your station,' I said.

'Thank goodness it's a short journey. I can't bear to sit in a train for more than two or three hours.'

Yet I was prepared to sit there for almost any length of time, just to listen to her talking. Her voice had the sparkle of a mountain stream. As soon as she left the train, she would forget our brief encounter; but it would stay with me for the rest of the journey, and for some time after.

The engine's whistle shrieked, the carriage wheels changed their sound and rhythm, the girl got up and began to collect her things. I wondered if she wore her hair in a bun, or if it was plaited; perhaps it was hanging loose over her shoulders, or was it cut very short?

The train drew slowly into the station. Outside, there was the shouting of porters and vendors and a high-pitched female voice near the carriage door; that voice must have belonged to the girl's aunt.

'Goodbye,' the girl said.

She was standing very close to me, so close that the perfume from her hair was tantalising. I wanted to raise my hand and touch her hair, but she moved away. Only the scent of perfume still lingered where she had stood.

There was some confusion in the doorway. A man, getting into the compartment, stammered an apology. Then the door banged, and the world was shut out again. I returned to my berth.

The guard blew his whistle and we moved off. Once again, I had a game to play and a new fellow-traveller.

The train gathered speed, the wheels took up their song, and the carriage groaned and shook. I found the window and sat in front of it, staring into the daylight that was darkness for me.

So many things were happening outside the window: it could be a fascinating game, guessing what went on out there.

The man who had entered the compartment broke into my reverie.

'You must be disappointed,' he said. 'I'm not nearly as attractive a travelling companion as the one who just left.'

'She was an interesting girl,' I said. 'Can you tell me—did she keep her hair long or short?'

'I don't remember,' he said, sounding puzzled. 'It was her eyes I noticed, not her hair. She had beautiful eyes—but they were of no use to her. She was completely blind. Didn't you notice?'

The Four Feathers

Our school dormitory was a very long room with about thirty beds, fifteen on either side of the room. This was good for pillow fights. Class V would take on Class VI (the two senior classes in our Prep school) and there would be plenty of space for leaping, struggling small boys, pillows flying, feathers flying, until there was a cry of 'Here comes Fishy!' or 'Here comes Olly!' and either Mr Fisher, the Headmaster, or Mr Oliver, the Senior Master, would come striding in, cane in hand, to put an end to the general mayhem.

Pillow fights were allowed, up to a point; nobody got hurt. But parents sometimes complained if, at the end of the term, a boy came home with a pillow devoid of cotton-wool or feathers.

In that last year at Prep school in Shimla, there were four of us who were close friends—Bimal, whose home was in Bombay; Riaz, who came from Lahore; Bran, who hailed from Vellore; and your narrator, who lived wherever his father (then in the Air Force) was posted.

We called ourselves the 'Four Feathers', the feathers signifying that we were companions in adventure, comrades-in-arms, and knights of the round table.

Bimal adopted a peacock's feather as his emblem—he was always a bit showy.

Riaz chose a falcon's feather—although we couldn't find one.

Bran and I were at first offered crows or murghi feathers, but we protested vigorously and threatened a walkout. Finally, I settled for a parrot's feather (taken from Mrs Fisher's pet parrot), and Bran found a woodpecker's, which suited him, as he was always knocking things about.

Bimal was all thin legs and arms, so light and frisky that at times he seemed to be walking on air. We called him 'Bambi', after the delicate little deer in the Disney film.

Riaz, on the other hand, was a sturdy boy, good at games though not very studious; but always good-natured, always smiling.

Bran was a dark, good-looking boy from the South; he was just a little spoilt—hated being given out in a cricket match and would refuse to leave the crease—but he was affectionate and a loyal friend.

I was the 'scribe'—good at inventing stories in order to get out of scrapes—but hopeless at sums, my highest marks being twenty-two out of one hundred.

On Sunday afternoons, when there were no classes or organised games, we were allowed to roam about on the hillside below the school.

The Four Feathers would laze about on the short summer grass, sharing the occasional food parcel from home, reading comics (sometimes a book), and making plans for the long winter holidays.

My father, who collected everything from stamps to seashells to butterflies, had given me a butterfly net and urged me to try and catch a rare species which, he said, was found only near Chotta Shimla.

He described it as a large purple butterfly with yellow and black borders on its wings. A Purple Emperor, I think it was called. As I wasn't very good at identifying

butterflies, I would chase anything that happened to flit across the school grounds, usually ending up with Common Red Admirals, Clouded Yellows, or Cabbage Whites. But that Purple Emperor—that rare specimen being sought by collectors the world over—proved elusive.

I would have to seek my fortune in some other line of endeavour.

One day, scrambling about among the rocks, and thorny bushes below the school, I almost fell over a small bundle lying in the shade of a young spruce tree. On taking a closer look, I discovered that the bundle was really a baby, wrapped up in a tattered old blanket.

'Feathers, feathers!' I called, 'Come here and look. A baby's been left here!'

The feathers joined me and we all stared down at the infant, who was fast asleep.

'Who would leave a baby on the hillside?' asked Bimal of no one in particular.

'Someone who doesn't want it,' said Bran.

'And hoped some good people would come along and keep it,' said Riaz.'

'A panther might have come along instead,' I said. 'Can't leave it here.'

'Well, we'll just have to adopt it,' said Bimal.

'We can't adopt a baby,' said Bran.

'Why not?'

'We have to be married.'

'We don't.'

'Not us, you dope. The grown-ups who adopt babies.'

'Well, we can't just leave it here for grows-ups to come along,' I said.

'We don't even know if it's a boy or a girl,' said Riaz.

'Makes no difference. A baby's a baby. Let's take it back to school.'

'And keep it in the dormitory?'

'Of course not. Who's going to feed it? Babies need milk. We'll hand it over to Mrs Fisher. She doesn't have a baby.'

'Maybe she doesn't want one. Look, it's beginning to cry. Let's hurry!'

Riaz picked up the wide-awake and crying baby and gave it to Bimal who gave it to Bran who gave it to me. The Four Feathers marched up the hill to school with a very noisy baby.

'Now it's done potty in the blanket,' I complained. 'And some, of it's on my shirt.'

'Never mind,' said Bimal. 'It's in a good cause. You're a Boy Scout, remember? You're supposed to help people in distress.'

The headmaster and his wife were in their drawing room, enjoying their afternoon tea and cakes. We trudged in, and Bimal announced, 'We've got something for Mrs Fisher.'

Mrs Fisher took one look at the bundle in my arms and let out a shriek. 'What have you brought here, Bond?'

'A baby, ma'am. I think it's a girl. Do you want to adopt it?'

Mrs Fisher threw up her arms in consternation, and turned to her husband. 'What are we to do, Frank? These boys are impossible. They've picked up someone's child!'

'We'll have to inform the police,' said Mr Fisher, reaching for the telephone. 'We can't have lost babies in the school.'

Just then there was a commotion outside, and a wild-eyed woman, her clothes dishevelled, entered at the front door accompanied by several menfolk from one of the villages. She ran towards us, crying out, 'My baby, my baby! *Mera bachcha*! You've stolen my baby!'

'We found it on the hillside,' I stammered. 'That's right,' said Bran. 'Finder's keepers!'

'Quiet, Adams,' said Mr Fisher, holding up his hand for order and addressing the villagers in a friendly manner. 'These boys found the baby alone on the hillside and brought it here before…before…'

'Before the hyenas got it,' I put in.

'Quite right, Bond. And why did you leave your child alone?' he asked the woman.

'I put her down for five minutes so that I could climb the plum tree and collect the plums. When I came down, the baby had gone! But I could hear it crying up on the hill. I called the menfolk and we come looking for it.'

'Well, here's your baby,' I said, thrusting it into her arms. By then I was glad to be rid of it! 'Look after it properly in future.'

'Kidnapper!' she screamed at me.

Mr Fisher succeeded in mollifying the villagers. 'These boys are good Scouts,' he told them. 'It's their business to help people.'

'Scout Law Number Three, sir,' I added. 'To be useful and helpful.'

And then the Headmaster turned the tables on the villagers. 'By the way, those plum trees belong to the school. So do the peaches and apricots. Now I know why they've been disappearing so fast!'

The villagers, a little chastened, went their way.

Mr Fisher reached for his cane. From the way he fondled it I knew he was

itching to use it on our bottoms.

'No, Frank,' said Mrs Fisher, intervening on our behalf. 'It was really very sweet of them to look after that baby.

'And look at Bond —he's got baby-goo all over his clothes.'

'So he has. Go and take a bath, all of you. And what are you grinning about, Bond?'

'Scout Law Number Eight, sir. A Scout smiles and whistles under all difficulties.'

And so ended the first adventure of the Four Feathers.

Our Great Escape

It had been a lonely winter for a fourteen-year-old. I had spent the first few weeks of the vacation with my mother and stepfather in Dehra.

Then they left for Delhi, and I was pretty much on my own. Of course, the servants were there to care for my needs, but there was no one to keep me company. I would wander off in the mornings, taking some path up the hills, come back home for lunch, read a bit and then stroll off again till it was time for dinner. Sometimes I walked up to my grandparents' house, but it seemed so different

now, with people I didn't know occupying the house.

With the three-month winter break over, I was almost eager to return to my boarding school in Shimla.

It wasn't as though I had many friends at school. I needed a friend but it was not easy to find one among a horde of rowdy, pea-shooting eighth formers, who carved their names on desks and stuck chewing gum on the class teacher's chair.

Had I grown up with other children, I might have developed a taste for schoolboy anarchy; but in sharing my father's loneliness after his separation from my mother, and in being bereft of any close family ties, I had turned into a premature adult.

After a month in the eighth form, I began to notice a new boy, Omar, and then only because he was a quiet, almost taciturn person who took no part in the form's feverish attempt to imitate the Marx Brothers at the circus. He showed no resentment at the prevailing anarchy, nor did he make a move to participate in it.

Once he caught me looking at him, and he smiled

ruefully, tolerantly. Did I sense another adult in the class? Someone who was a little older than his years?

Even before we began talking to each other, Omar and I developed an understanding of sorts, and we'd nod almost respectfully to each other when we met in the classroom corridors or the environs of the dining hall or the dormitory.

We were not in the same house. The house system practised its own form of apartheid, whereby a member of one house was not expected to fraternise with someone belonging to another.

Those public schools certainly knew how to clamp you into compartments. However, these barriers vanished when Omar and I found ourselves selected for the School Colts' hockey team, Omar as a full-back, I as the goalkeeper.

The taciturn Omar now spoke to me occasionally, and we combined well on the field of play. A good understanding is needed between a goalkeeper and a full-back. We were on the same wavelength.

I anticipated his moves, he was familiar with mine. Years later, when I read Conrad's The Secret Sharer, I thought of Omar.

It wasn't until we were away from the confines of school, classroom and dining hall that our friendship flourished. The hockey team travelled to Sanawar on the next mountain range, where we were to play a couple of matches against our old rivals, the Lawrence Royal Military School.

This had been my father's old school, so I was keen to explore its grounds and peep into its classrooms.

Omar and I were thrown together a good deal during the visit to Sanawar, and in our more leisurely moments, strolling undisturbed around a school where we were guests and not pupils, we exchanged life histories and other confidences.

Omar, too, had lost his father—had I sensed that before? Shot in some tribal encounter on the Frontier, for he hailed from the lawless lands beyond Peshawar.

A wealthy uncle saw to Omar's education.

We wandered into the school chapel, and there I found my father's name—A. A. Bond—on the school's roll of honour board: old boys who had lost their lives while serving during the two World Wars.

'What did his initials stand for?' asked Omar.

'Aubrey Alexander.'

'Unusual names, like yours. Why did your parents call you Rusty?'

'I am not sure.' I told him about the book I was writing. It was my first one and was called Nine Months (the length of the school term, not a pregnancy), and it described some of the happenings at school and lampooned a few of our teachers.

I had filled three slim exercise books with this premature literary project, and I allowed Omar to go through them. He must have been my first reader and critic.

'They're very interesting,' he said, 'but you'll get into trouble if someone finds them, especially Mr Fisher.'

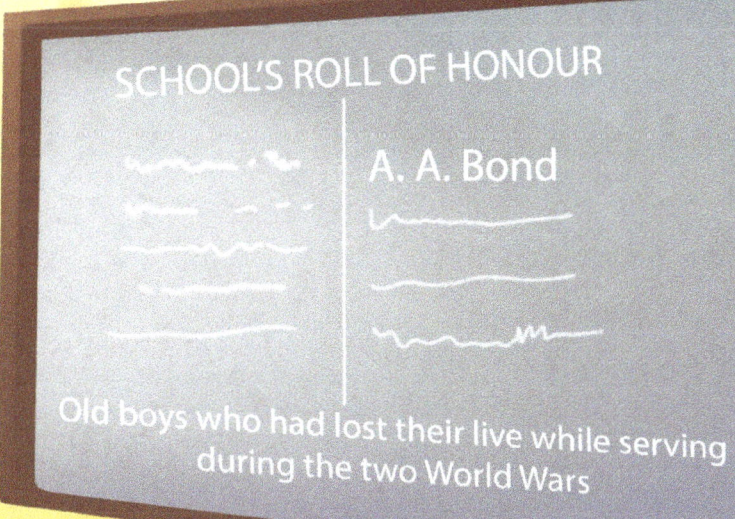

SCHOOL'S ROLL OF HONOUR

A. A. Bond

Old boys who had lost their live while serving during the two World Wars

I have to admit it wasn't great literature. I was better at hockey and football. I made some spectacular saves, and we won our matches against Sanawar. When we returned to Shimla, we were school heroes for a couple of days and lost some of our reticence; we were even a little more forthcoming with other boys.

And then Mr Fisher, my housemaster, discovered my literary opus, Nine Months, under my mattress, and took it away and read it (as he told me later) from cover to cover. Corporal punishment

then being in vogue, I was given six of the best with a springy Malacca cane, and my manuscript was torn up and thrown into Mr Fisher's wastepaper basket. All I had to show for my efforts were some purple welts on my bottom. These were proudly displayed to all who were interested, and I was a hero for another two days.

'Will you go away too when the British leave India?' Omar asked me one day.

'I don't think so,' I said. 'I don't have anyone to go back to in England, and my guardian, Mr Harrison, too seems to have no intention of going back.'

'Everyone is saying that our leaders and the British are going to divide the country. Shimla will be in India, Peshawar in Pakistan!'

'Oh, it won't happen,' I said glibly. 'How can they cut up such a big country?' But even as we chatted about the possibility, Nehru, Jinnah and Mountbatten, and all those who mattered, were preparing their instruments for major surgery.

Before their decision impinged on our lives and everyone else's, we found a little freedom of our own, in an underground tunnel that we discovered below the third flat.

It was really part of an old, disused drainage

system, and when Omar and I began exploring it, we had no idea just how far it extended.

After crawling along on our bellies for some twenty feet, we found ourselves in complete darkness. Omar had brought along a small pencil torch, and with its help we continued writhing forward (moving backwards would have been quite impossible) until we saw a glimmer of light at the end of the tunnel.

Dusty, musty, very scruffy, we emerged at last onto a grassy knoll, a little way outside the school boundary.

It's always a great thrill to escape beyond the boundaries that adults have devised. Here we were in unknown territory. To travel without passports—that would be the ultimate freedom!

But more passports were on their way—and more boundaries.

Lord Mountbatten, viceroy and governor-general-to-be, came for our Founder's Day and gave away the prizes. I had won a prize for something or the other, and mounted the rostrum to receive my book from this towering, handsome man in his pinstripe suit.

Bishop Cotton's was then the premier school in India, often referred to as the 'Eton of the East'.

Viceroys and governors had graced its functions. Many of its boys had gone on to eminence in the civil services and armed forces. There was one 'old boy' about whom they maintained

a stolid silence—General Dyer, who had ordered the massacre at Amritsar and destroyed the trust that had been building up between Britain and India.

Now Mountbatten spoke of the momentous events that were happening all around us—the War had just come to an end, the United Nations held out the promise of a world living in peace and harmony, and India, an equal partner with Britain, would be among the great nations...

A few weeks later, Bengal and the Punjab provinces were bisected. Riots flared up across northern India, and there was a great exodus of people crossing the newly-drawn frontiers of Pakistan and India. Homes were destroyed, thousands lost their lives.

The common room radio and the occasional newspaper kept us abreast of events, but in our tunnel, Omar and I felt immune from all that was happening, worlds away from all the pillage, murder and revenge.

And outside the tunnel, on the pine knoll below the school, there was fresh untrodden grass, sprinkled with clover and daisies; the only sounds we heard were the hammering of a woodpecker and the distant insistent call of the Himalayan

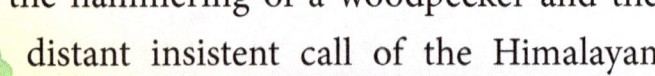

Barbet. Who could touch us there?

'And when all the wars are done,' I said, 'a butterfly will still be beautiful.'

'Did you read that somewhere?'

'No, it just came into my head.'

'Already you're a writer.'

'No, I want to play hockey for India or football for Arsenal. Only winning teams!'

'You can't win forever. Better to be a writer.'

When the monsoon arrived, the tunnel was flooded, the drain choked with rubble.

We were allowed out to the cinema to see Laurence Olivier's Hamlet, a film that did nothing

to raise our spirits on a wet and gloomy afternoon; but it was our last picture that year, because communal riots suddenly broke out in Shimla's Lower Bazaar, an area that was still much as Kipling had described it—'a man who knows his way there can defy all the police of India's summer capital'—and we were confined to school indefinitely.

One morning after prayers in the chapel, the headmaster announced that the Muslim boys—those who had their homes in what was now

Pakistan—would have to be evacuated, sent to their homes across the border with an armed convoy.

The tunnel no longer provided an escape for us. The bazaar was out of bounds. The flooded playing field was deserted. Omar and I sat on a damp wooden bench and talked about the future in vaguely hopeful terms, but we didn't solve any problems. Mountbatten and Nehru and Jinnah were doing all the solving.

It was soon time for Omar to leave—he left along with some fifty other boys from Lahore, Pindi and Peshawar. The rest of us—Hindus, Christians, Parsis—helped them load their luggage into the waiting trucks.

A couple of boys broke down and wept. So did our departing school captain, a Pathan who had been known for his stoic and unemotional demeanour. Omar waved cheerfully to me and I waved back. We had vowed to meet again some day.

The convoy got through safely enough. There was only one casualty—the school cook, who had strayed into an off-limits area in the foothill town of Kalika and been set upon by a mob. He wasn't seen again.

Towards the end of the school year, just as we were all getting ready to leave for the school holidays, I received a letter from Omar.

He told me something about his new school and how he missed my company and our games and our tunnel to freedom. I replied and gave him my home address, but I did not hear from him again. Some seventeen or eighteen years later, I did get news of Omar, but in an entirely different context. India and Pakistan were at war, and in a bombing raid over Ambala, not far from Shimla, a Pakistani plane was shot down. Its crew died in the crash.

One of them, I learnt later, was Omar.

Did he, I wonder, get a glimpse of the playing fields we knew so well as boys? Perhaps memories of his schooldays flooded back as he flew over the foothills. Perhaps he remembered the tunnel through which we were able to make our little escape to freedom.

But there are no tunnels in the sky.

The Night Train at Deoli

When I was at college, I used to spend my summer vacations in Dehra, at my grandmother's place. I would leave the plains early in May and return late in July. Deoli was a small station about thirty miles from Dehra. It marked the beginning of the heavy jungles of the Indian Terai.

The train would reach Deoli at about five in the morning when the station would be dimly lit with electric bulbs and oil lamps, and the jungle across the railway tracks would just be visible in the faint light of dawn. Deoli had only one platform, an office for the Stationmaster and a waiting room.

The platform boasted a tea stall, a fruit vendor and a few stray dogs; not much else because the train stopped there for only ten minutes before rushing on into the forests.

Why it stopped at Deoli, I don't know. Nothing ever happened there. Nobody got off the train and nobody got on. There were never any coolies on the platform. But the train would halt there a full ten minutes and then a bell would sound, the guard would blow his whistle, and presently Deoli would be left behind and forgotten.

I used to wonder what happened in Deoli behind the station walls. I always felt sorry for that lonely little

platform and for the place that nobody wanted to visit. I decided that one day I would get off the train at Deoli and spend the day there just to please the town.

I was eighteen, visiting my grandmother, and the night train stopped at Deoli. A girl came down the platform selling baskets.

It was a cold morning and the girl had a shawl thrown across her shoulders. Her feet were bare and her clothes were old but she was a young girl, walking gracefully and with dignity.

When she came to my window, she stopped. She saw that I was looking at her intently, but at first she pretended not to notice. She had pale skin, set off by shiny black hair and dark, troubled eyes. And then those eyes, searching and eloquent, met mine.

She stood by my window for some time and neither of us said anything. But when she moved on, I found myself leaving my seat and going to the carriage door. I stood waiting on the platform looking the other way.

I walked across to the tea stall. A kettle was boiling over on a small fire, but the owner of the stall was busy serving tea somewhere on the train.

The girl followed me behind the stall.

'Do you want to buy a basket?' she asked. 'They are very strong, made of the finest cane…'

'No,' I said, 'I don't want a basket.'

We stood looking at each other for what seemed a very long time, and she said, 'Are you sure you don't want a basket?'

'All right, give me one,' I said, and took the one on top and gave her a rupee, hardly daring to touch her fingers.

As she was about to speak, the guard blew his whistle. She said something, but it was lost in the clanging of the bell and the hissing of the engine. I had to run back to my compartment. The carriage shuddered and jolted forward.

I watched her as the platform slipped away. She was alone on the platform and she did not move, but she was looking at me and smiling. I watched her until the signal box came in the way and then the jungle hid the station. But I could still see her standing there alone…

I stayed awake for the rest of the journey. I could not rid my mind of the picture of the girl's face and her dark, smouldering eyes.

But when I reached Dehra, the incident became blurred and distant, for there were other things to occupy my mind. It was only when I was making the return journey, two months later, that I remembered the girl.

I was looking out for her as the train drew into the station, and I felt an unexpected thrill when I saw her walking up the platform. I sprang off the footboard and waved to her.

When she saw me, she smiled. She was pleased that I remembered her. I was pleased that she remembered me. We were both pleased and it was almost like a meeting of old friends.

She did not go down the length of the train selling baskets but came straight to the tea stall. Her dark eyes were suddenly filled with light. We said nothing for some time but we couldn't have been more eloquent.

I felt the impulse to put her on the train there and then, and take her away with me. I could not bear the thought of having to watch her recede into the distance of Deoli station. I took the baskets from her hand and put them down on the ground. She put out her hand for one of them, but I caught her hand and held it.

'I have to go to Delhi,' I said.

She nodded. 'I do not have to go anywhere.'

The guard blew his whistle for the train to leave, and how I hated the guard for doing that.

'I will come again,' I said. 'Will you be here?'

She nodded again and, as she nodded, the bell clanged and the train slid forward. I had to wrench my hand away from the girl and run for the moving train.

This time I did not forget her. She was with me for the remainder of the journey and for long after. All that year she was a bright, living thing. And when the college term finished, I packed in haste and left for Dehra earlier than usual. My grandmother would be pleased with my eagerness to see her.

I was nervous and anxious as the train drew into Deoli, because I was wondering what I should say to the girl and what I should do. I was determined that I wouldn't stand helplessly before her, hardly able to speak or do anything about my feelings.

The train came to Deoli, and I looked up and down the platform but I could not see the girl anywhere.

I opened the door and stepped off the footboard. I was deeply disappointed and overcome by a sense of foreboding. I felt I had to do something and so I ran up to the Stationmaster and said, 'Do you know the girl who used to sell baskets here?'

'No, I don't,' said the Stationmaster.

'And you'd better get on the train if you don't want to be left behind.'

But I paced up and down the platform and stared over the railings at the station yard. All I saw was a mango tree and a dusty road leading into the jungle. Where did the road go? The train was moving out of the station and I had to run up the platform and jump for the door of my compartment. Then, as the train gathered speed and rushed through the forests, I sat brooding in front of the window.

What could I do about finding a girl I had seen only twice, who had hardly spoken to me, and about whom I knew nothing—absolutely nothing— but for whom I felt a tenderness and responsibility that I had never felt before?

My grandmother was not pleased with my visit after all, because, I didn't stay at her place more than a couple of weeks. I felt restless and ill at ease. So I took the train back to the plains, meaning to ask further questions of the Stationmaster at Deoli.

But at Deoli, there was a new Stationmaster. The previous man had been transferred to another post within the past week. The new man didn't know anything about the girl who sold baskets. I found the owner of the tea stall, a small, shrivelled-up man, wearing greasy clothes, and asked him if he knew anything about the girl with the baskets.

'Yes, there was such a girl here. I remember quite well,' he said. 'But she has stopped coming now.'

'Why?' I asked. 'What happened to her?' 'How should I know?' said the man. 'She was nothing to me.' And once again, I had to run for the train. As Deoli platform receded, I decided that one day I would have to break journey there, spend a day in the town, make inquiries, and find the girl who had stolen my heart with nothing but a look from her dark, impatient eyes.

With this thought I consoled myself throughout my last term in college. I went to Dehra again in the summer and when, in the early hours of the morning, the night train drew into Deoli station, I looked up and down the platform for signs of the girl, knowing I wouldn't find her but hoping just the same.

Somehow, I couldn't bring myself to break journey at Deoli and spend a day there. (If it was all fiction or a film, I reflected, I would have got down and cleaned up the mystery and reached a suitable ending to the whole thing.)

I think I was afraid to do this. I was afraid of discovering what really happened to the girl. Perhaps she was no longer in Deoli, perhaps she was married, perhaps she had fallen ill…

In the last few years I have passed through Deoli many times, and I always look out of the carriage window half expecting to see the same unchanged face smiling up at me. I wonder what happens in Deoli, behind the station walls.

But I will never break my journey there. It may spoil my game. I prefer to keep hoping and dreaming and looking out of the window up and down that lonely platform, waiting for the girl with the baskets.

I never break my journey at Deoli but I pass through as often as I can.